THE GO CLUB

BY CAROL NICKLAUS

SILVER PRESS

Library of Congress Cataloging-in-Publication Data
Nicklaus, Carol.
   The GO Club / by Carol Nicklaus.
      p. cm.
   Summary: Young cats ride their bikes to the park, observ-
ing safety practices on the way.
   [1. Bicycles and bicycling--Fiction. 2. Cats--Fiction.]
I. Title.
PZ7.N5583Go 1991
[E]--dc20   Roader   91-13357
                        (Yellow Dot)   CIP
                                                      AC
ISBN 0-671-73500-4 (LSB)   ISBN 0-671-73505-5

Published by Silver Press, a division of
Silver Burdett Press, Inc.
Simon & Schuster, Inc.
Prentice Hall Bldg., Englewood Cliffs, NJ 07632.
Printed in the United States of America.
10   9   8   7   6   5   4   3   2   1

I like to ride
my big red bike.
I will ride my bike
to the bike parade.

We all have bikes
and we all will ride.
It will be a great parade!

I take care of my bike.

I put oil on the chain.

I put air in the tires.

I want my bike to work.

I check the brakes.

I look at the spokes.

I wash my bike, too.

It will look great
in the bike parade!

The bike parade
will be in the park,
and I know the way
to the park.

I go over the bridge,
and under the trees,
and down the path
to the park.

I watch out for rocks
or for holes in the road.

And leaves and mud
can be slippery.

I won't get lost.

I won't get stuck.

And I will ride my bike

in the bike parade.

My new blue bike
has two big wheels,
and two little wheels
so I won't fall down.

I know the rules
when I ride my bike.

Red light—I stop.

Green light—I can go.

Left hand out—
I turn left.

Left hand up—
I turn right.

Left hand down
when I want to stop.

And I always ride
on the right!

My pedal feels loose.
I can fix it
with my wrench.

Now I made the pedal tight.

I am on my way

to the bike parade.

I rode over the bridge
and under the trees.
Now where is the path
to the park?

Oh! I see the path.
I can ride down the path
and all the way
to the bike parade.

The light is red.

I have to stop.

I have to wait

to cross the street.

Now the light is green.

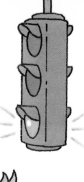

I can go.

I can ride my bike

to the bike parade.

I had to stop
to fix my bike.

I had to look
to find the path.

The light was red

so I had to wait.

Now the GO Club is here.

We can start the bike parade.

Hey! Wait for me!

Can I ride with you?

You can ride
with the GO Club, too!

One wheel.

Two wheels.

Three wheels.

Four wheels.

The GO Club likes
all kinds of bikes.

Look at the GO Club go!

TIRE TALK

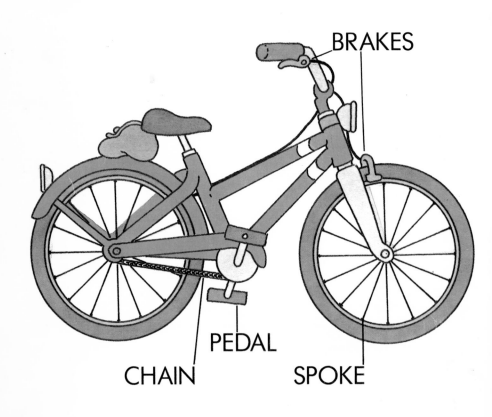

BRAKES

PEDAL

CHAIN   SPOKE